Dagger of the Heart

JOYCE NEWBERRY

Dagger of the Heart
Copyright © 2025 by Joyce Newberry

Library of Congress Control Number: 2025909144

ISBN
979-8-89641-069-0 (Paperback)
979-8-89641-070-6 (eBook)
979-8-89641-068-3 (Hardcover)

Table of Contents

ove has no boundaries for Rei who search for a woman who he never suspected is right in front of him. Markita felt love was out of bounds she met a man who she really did not know but accepts her completely. It happens when we need love to pick our hearts up to brings life into our soul.

One dark and foggy night in Fallacy City a pretty, woman was driving home two blocks away from her house when she saw a shadow laying on the street. He appeared to be lying in front of her head in front of her headlights. She stops her car to see if he was unconsciousness after swerving to avoid hitting him and almost runs into a ditch. She climbs out to try to wake him but got no response, but she did check his pulse. He is alive as she notices he had shoulder length, black hair with a mustache. She noticed his facial features resembled a Japanese man. He appeared to be 5'11" tall and around 35 years old just before checked his right jacket pocket to see he has a black, snakeskin wallet. She opens his wallet to see a state driver license stating his name is Rei Nakatani. He lives only two blocks from her home. Her name is Markita Brahman, a pretty, single African American woman. She decided to put him into her black 2019 Chevy Impala. He was heavy but she manages to maneuver him into her gray, passenger seat. She pulled up into her lighted driveway and pushed the garage remote. The garage door opened slowly, and she pulled in, but he did not move at all. She climbs out the car and walked toward the passenger side. She lifted him up to place his right hand on her shoulder. She brought him inside her one level home. She removed his black leather jacket in her beige guestroom. It had beige and gold print curtains. He was wearing a white shirt with black slacks. She placed him on the bed to untie his white laces, and remove his black, athletics shoes. She took off his socks and lifted his right pants leg. You have nice legs. She walked toward the door but turned to stare at him. She shook her head in disbelief of meeting an attractive man in this manner before closing the door. She walked into her yellow, kitchen to get a glass of juice. She looked at the gold tone, clock on her wall and it showed 9:30 p.m. She was thinking to herself; I hope he is not a pervert. She is 26 years of age who does not have a husband or children. She recently broke up with her ex-boyfriend of ten years. She stands 5'8" tall with brown eyes and wavy dark brown hair that hangs to her shoulders. She walks into her bathroom to remove her clothes. Markita thinks about how she almost hits this handsome man. She pulls the pink and burgundy sheer curtain back. She climbs into the bathtub and turns on the stainless steel, faucet handles. She leans her head forward to let the water run down her body leaving water beads. Her unconscious guest was standing there with a lilac, towel as he wrapped, it around her gently. "I didn't mean to startled you." He could see fear written on her face. She trembled a little when his hands graze her shoulders. "I thought you were asleep!" He stared into her pretty, brown eyes with a smile adorning his handsome face. "The water from your shower woke me." "I'm sorry!" "Thanks for helping me!" "No problem!" "My name is Rei." "My name is Markita." They shook hands with each other. "I'll let you get dress then we can talk." "Fine!" He left her alone to walked into the living room while she entered her bedroom. She slipped into a peach nightgown with matching robe and walked into the living room. He traced up her body slowly with his eyes but smile at her. She sat down on her soft, blue leather love seat. He sat across from her on the couch. "What were you doing out on the road when I saw you?" "I was running from some guys." "I had a run in at a bar." "Were they harassing you?" "Yes, they didn't like my skin tone." "There are jerks everywhere." "True, you are not threatening by my skin?"

He waited to hear her say what he assumed she would say. "No, I believe everyone should be treated fairly regardless of color." "That noble but unfortunately everyone does not share your viewpoint." "Do you want anything to drink?" "Do you have any juice or water?" He was not sure what to make of this beauty that rescued him. She seemed genuine but thought that it was an act. "Yes, juice if that is okay!" She walked into the kitchen and he followed her. He could have taken her at the drop of the hat without resistance. She is guarded by his presence in her home. She turned around to hand him a glass, but he was standing in front of her. "You are very pretty." "Thanks!" He could see her attraction to him, but she turns away from his eye contact. "I would like to repay you." "You don't have to do that." "I insist!" Their eyes lock on one another for a moment. He drank his juice and placed it on the cabinet. "May I stay in your guest room until morning?" "Yes, good-night Rei! "Goodnight Markita!" She heard him closed the door and climbs into bed to turned off the light. Rei removed his shirt and pants and pulled the covers back. He slides down in bed and thinks about her. You are quite a woman Markita, I must know more about you. I could not help myself from staring at your beautiful body. He turned his light off and drifted to sleep. She awoke screaming at 4:00 a.m., and he ran into her room wearing only a black pair of underwear. "What's the matter?" "I had a nightmare." She appeared to be flustered and sweating a bit on her forehead. "You want to talk about it?" "No!" He could sense her reluctance to talk about it as she tried not to stare at him. He sat on the edge of the bed but caressed her face. She moves away from his hand to climb out of bed. He could not help staring at her pink nightgown as it clings to her breasts. "Try to get some sleep!" "I will try." He turned around to glance at her before leaving her room. He was wondering what was troubling her. He lay down thinking of her before falling asleep. She lay down to drifted asleep within minutes.

He awoke the next morning to take a shower almost bumped into her as he exits the bathroom. I am sorry!" "It's all right!" He had a gray towel wrapped around his waist. She turned away when she gazed at Rei strong, muscular shoulders. He starred into her pretty, brown eyes and smiled at her. "There's no need to be embarrassed." She just closes the bathroom door. Baby, we will get to know one another better. She closed her eyes and felt the water rinse soap from her body. She pulled the curtain back to step out this time no Rei. He buttoned his shirt and imagined her in his arms. He opened the stainless-steel refrigerator door in the kitchen and to see the orange juice. He poured up the juice in two, light green, plastic tumblers. She slipped on a plum, skirt with a light plum, blouse. It outlined her shape of her nipples protruding from her bra. Her hair was placed in a ponytail but left the rest hanging down in the back. She felt his eyes tracing up her body when he handed her the tumbler but almost dropped it. "I didn't mean to make you nervous by my staring." "It is okay!" "Can you drive me home?" "I stay a couple blocks from here." She walked into her living room to retrieve his black, leather jacket. They put on their coats before walking out her red door. She pulled up in the driveway of a hunter green two-story house. It had a 2018 dark blue, car in the driveway. "Your car?" "That's right!" "That's a

BMW, right?" "You know cars." "Yes, only certain ones!" She followed him inside and closed the door behind her. She stares at his tan living room with dark gray vertical blinds and large sectional with nice glass lamps. "You want something to drink?" "No thanks! "Nice place you have here." "It is home!" "May I take your coat?" She unbuttoned her coat and handed it to him. He hung it up on a gold coat rack. She sat down on his Italian, black leather couch.

"I will be right back." He walked upstairs to his bedroom to remove his shirt. He looked through his walk-in closet and found a pair of blue jeans and a gray T-shirt. He held a Herringbone, 24kt gold chain in his left hand. He walked downstairs to gazed at her.

"Can I trouble you to help me?" "Sure!" She stood up as she placed the chain around his neck. Her arms around were still around his neck while caressing her face Thanks!" He started to kiss her but decided that this is not the right moment.

"What do you do for a living?" "I worked at the Night Flight nightclub." "I'm a bouncer for Mr. Richard Van Carver." "I heard of him!" "He is an Import/Export, businessman."

"He has money?" "Yes, he owns the club." "Are you married?" "No, are you dating anyone?" "No, that is too bad!" He smiles at her. "I have to go." His questions were getting too personal. She was about to leave as he stopped her after giving her coat back. "Markita can I ask you a question?" "Yes!" "What do you do for a living?"

"I'm an Interior Decorator." "Maybe, I will hire you to decorate my den." "I can do that."

She took a pink and gray business card out her purse as she handed it to him. He glances at the card to see a picture of her on it. "Now I can say I know an Interior Decorator." He escorted her to his front oak door. "Is it all right if I call you sometime?" "Okay!" She agreed to left but drove away.

Checking Out Her Workplace

e can be friends now but one day we will be lovers. He realized that Markita legal lifestyle will not compare to his. He picked up his silver phone as he calls Mr. Van Carver. "It is me!" "Did you complete your assignment?" "Yes, just as you ordered." "Good, come to the club tonight at 6:00 p.m. "I will be there." Rei clicked off the telephone and sat down on his black, soft velvet couch. He focuses on the lady who rescued him. He drove past her house but no car but pulled out her business card. Her office was located downtown which was fifteen minutes away. He walked in to ask to see her from the receptionist. Her building looked very modern with the name "Fresh Interior Designers Serves You" There were three other Interior Designers plus a Receptionist and Manager. It was well lit with black leather chairs in every office with laptops. He walks toward a woman who appeared to be twenty-five years old. She was the same height as Markita she stood up with black hair, green eyes. He did tell her that he is a client. She "Markita there's a new client here to see you." She pushed a button on the phone. He could see she was a cheerful person. She escorted him to her office. "Thank you, Lindsey!" Lindsey left out the door while he walked into her office. "Nice to see you again!" "Rei what are you doing here?" He stood there wearing a pair of dark blue dress pants and a white shirt. "I am here to offer you work." "You want me to decorate your study." "Yes!" He stared at her smiling face. "When do you want me to start?" "How about tomorrow morning at 10:00 a.m.?" "Okay!" "You can stop by this afternoon at 5:00 p.m." "To take a closer look at the room." "I will call to confirm." They agreed and he left her office. Lindsey walked back into her office and smiled at her. "What?" "Who's the handsome stranger?" "A new client." "He seems to be taken with you." She smiles at her noticing the redness showing in her face. "You better watch him." "He might have designs on you." "All right!" Lindsey enjoys teasing her friend knowing she has not dated much.

Markita remembered Rei caressing her face. He has strong, gentle hands and beautiful eyes. She finished working on a design for another client's house before leaving the office. She got into her car and drove to this condominium building in town. He followed two cars behind her to the Perlis flower shop. He purchased a dozen, long stem red roses to give to her. He planned to charm her into his arms and his bed. He could taste intimacy with her at his side. He glanced at his Sterling Silver; Rolex watch to drive toward his brother's house. He lives in this tan two-story brick house that had three bedrooms, one and half bathrooms, finished basement, open plan living room that follows into the kitchen. It has a two-car garage, but this was left by their dad who died of a stroke. He left the house to my brother which I the will left me his BMW. "What is up brother?" "I am on my way to work!" "Are you staying out of trouble?" "Of course!" Chris Nakatani is his half-brother. "Trouble is not my middle name." They have the same father but different mothers. He is a 40-year-old, White man with sandy brown hair and green eyes. Chris stands 6'1" tall with a medium build. His job occupation is an Accounting Manager at an accounting firm which means he wears dress pants and shirts five days a week. "You found yourself a woman yet?" "I met this pretty woman named Markita." "What is her race?" "Does that really matter?" "You know society is going to judge you no matter what. "She is African-American!" "Why you cannot you find a nice Asian woman." "You sound like our mother!" Rei shakes his head in disbelief over his brother last comment. "He knew where this is leading to but was not ready to hear that!"

"She isn't like any woman I ever met; my skin tone is not an issue." He remembers how she responded to seeing him in just a towel. Our lips almost tasted one another. "Oh really, she is rare!" "That's why I plan on making her mine." He had this devious look on his face like a cat that swallowed a canary. "Be nice not letting your animal instinct kick in." "I am always a gentleman to the ladies and this one is different." "How many have you brought home?" "No one since Michelle." "She had possibilities." "You are looking at her Asian skin." "She was fooling around with her boss." "This woman what do you know about her?" "She is an Interior Decorator who drives a 2018 black Chevy Impala; I know where the lady resides." "Nice gas saving car!" "How did you manage that?" His face showed surprise that his brother knew all that about this woman. "I have my little secrets." "I will let you get back to work." "Yeah, it is 12:55 p.m."

Rei jumped into his car to head back to his house where he placed the red roses, he purchases to place into a crystal vase with some water. He was imagining her face. He thought about how he was deceiving his brother and his so-to-be woman on what he did for a living. He planned to tell her the truth one-day but after she belongs to him. We would explore every aspect of passion to relentless heights of passion. Society is not our obstacle but our strength.

She took a late lunch at 2:00 p.m., and Lindsey joined her in her Chevy Impala at the San Maria it was a Mexican restaurant. They stopped at a deli shop to pick up a salad to go. "You better watch yourself around Rei." Lindsey has worked with her for several years. She is a 25-year-old White woman with black hair, past her shoulder length green eyes who stands 5'8 at 127 lbs. Her rose blouse, gray shirt and gray heels kept her looking professional. "Rei is a nice man." "Yeah, it will be nice to hit the sheets with him." Lindsey gets your mind out of the bedroom." "Do you find him attractive?" "Yes, but he is a client." "You can mix business with pleasure, I would." "You play your cards right you can get paid too." "I would be playing with fire; I do not have one-night stands." Her face registers seriousness at that thought. She knew she would want more than just that from him.

They arrived back at the office around 3:00 p.m. She walked out the office at 4:55 p.m. to drive to his house within fifteen minutes. She walked up to his door and he opened it. "I am running a little late, sorry." Rei took her coat to give her a tour of his upstairs. He took her into his den not forgetting how much he wants her at his side. "What do you think?" She seen a den that looked plain without furniture or anything in it.

"It could use some sprucing up." "Some color painted on a wall that would accent the office furniture. How about a nice bookcase with a sofa and, a small desk if you like?" "That sounds interesting, you have good ideas." He walked behind her into the guestroom next to it. She looked around the room and turned to talk to him. He was standing in front of her. She could smell the cologne on his neck as he stood close to her. "Your cologne smells nice." "Thank you!" She got nervous from his roaming eyes. "What do you have in mind?" "Can you design these two rooms, paint, furniture everything?" "Okay, what colors, furniture design do you like?" He smiles at her. "Maybe we can discuss this tomorrow at the club I work for Night Flight around 9:00 p.m.?" "Not tonight!" How about tomorrow at 10:00 am?" "See you tomorrow morning." He escorted her back downstairs and she left him.

Finished Business

He knew he had an appointment to be to 6:30 p.m. There were only fifteen minutes as he glanced at his silver Rolex watch to get to the club to meet Mr. Van Carver. He knew he was a stickler for being on time. He climbed into his car and drove to the Night Flight. He was sitting at a back table with his back to the wall. The club seemed to be jumping with the red suede chairs with black tables that had silver napkin holders with salt and pepper shakers next to the napkins. The round tables were big enough to sit four guests but there were eight booth tables on other side. They had red backing with black tables with the same napkins and salt n pepper shakers too. Guests could order food from the kitchen which includes chicken sliders, mozzarella sticks, beef nachos, hot wings, fries, and a variety of juices, wine coolers beer and can soft drinks. The bar was for guests who were alone which seated 12 but alcoholic drinks. There was no Whiskey or beer serve just Tequila, Daquiri, and seven fruity drinks too. The flashing dance floor was large enough to hold at least fifty people. The disco ball did not represent eighties music but mostly 2000 and current music. There was a D.J. stand where songs could be requested. "You're late!" He was angry at him. "You have something for me?" He passed Rei a silver attaché briefcase under the table. "You have another job for me?" Mr. Van Carver is a fifty-five old White male who has a mustache is starting to show his age. His eyes have deep circle under them, and he seem like he used to be in shape but started getting a stomach from lack of exercise and heavy drinking. He was wearing a black suit which he handed him a large, manila envelope. He opened the brown envelope to see picture of a White male who looked to be 50 years old with graying hair. Rei placed it back in the envelope but got up to leave. "I want to know everything about him." "Eat and stay for a while." Rei realize he sometime indulge his boss. He ordered three chicken sliders and an order of mozzarella sticks and a wine cooler. He got up to leave. "Stay and find some woman to dance with." "Not tonight, I just want to go home and get some rest." He walked out with the envelope under his arm. He climbed into his BMW turned the key on thinking about Markita. He pulled off to reach his house with in twenty minutes. He picked up his phone to see it read about 9:30 p.m. He wanted to see her tonight but instead choose not to disturb her. He decided to text her that he will see her tomorrow at 10:00 a.m. She responded back okay.

Markita awoke at 8:00 a.m., sat up in her bed. She wrapped her Aztec sheet around herself and daydreamed about Rei. She stood to her feet and dropped the sheet on the floor. She goes take a shower with thoughts of Rei. She put on a light, jade suede suit and an ivory blouse underneath it. She placed her hair in a ponytail and called into work. "Lindsey, I will be into work in the afternoon." She walked into the kitchen to get a glass of juice and the telephone ring startled her. "Hello!" "Markita it's me!" "Rei!" "I will be over at 10:00 a.m." "I called to see if you had anymore nightmares." "No! She knew the real reason he called her. "See you in an hour." She felt herself giving in to passion. "I have a job to do, and I will do it." Time was moving rather quickly, it was now 9:30 a.m. She stared into the mirror but took a deep breath before locking her door at 9:50 a.m. He opened the door before she knocked on the door. She moved past him but tried to not stare in his eyes. He removed her coat and smiled at her. "You are so beautiful." "He showed her your study first sounding serious. She avoids any conversation with him. He escorted her upstairs and pointed out his bedroom to her. He led her inside his den. "What kind of changes are you looking for?" "What do you suggest?" He gave her the once over. You could change from curtains to vertical blinds, adding new carpet and painting the wall a lighter color with one accent wall. "Do you like warm colors like brown, red, oranges or green? He could not stop staring at her pretty legs. She turned away from him to avoid his stare. She could see he focus on her. He walked in front of her to caress her right cheek. "You ready to check out the guest room?" "Alright, lead the "way." He showed her the guest bedroom, and it was light gray next to his bedroom. It was plain but it did have a full-size bed in the room with dark blue sheets on the bed, and it looked lifeless. "I want you decorate this room personally." "Whatever you suggest. "I will pay the cost." She stared up into his piercing eyes. He walked toward her to kisses her lips fully. "You are a client; I don't mix business with pleasure." He pulled her into his arms as she trembled in his arms. "I do not have to be your client if it will keep us apart." "What do you want from me?" "For us to be lovers!" "I want you baby." She sat down on the bed next to him. "It will be good between us." He placed his hand under her chin to meet his stare. "I don't know!" She placed her hands on his strong, muscular shoulders to stroke them. "No, I can't Rei!" She stood up and started to bolt out the door, but he grabbed her arm to gently pulled her into his arms. He kisses her lips as her breathing became heavy. She stroked his shoulder length black hair as he took her hair a loose. He moved her beautiful, dark brown, hair toward her face. He started to unbutton her light jade suit jacket as he touches her face. "Can we take things more slowly?" He stops to stare at her. "Okay, maybe I am coming on too strong." "I am attracted to you." "Just let us get to know each other better." Rei buttoned the one button he unbuttoned. He kisses her as he walks her to his door. "Can we go out tonight as friends?" "I will call you after 5:00 pm." He caresses her face as he gives her a brief kiss. "Think about us alright!" "Okay!" He watched her walk toward her Impala and drive away.

He realized that he is getting under Markita's skin. You are going to taste my passion very soon. He looks through his closet decides to put on a dark blue suit which he lays across his bed. He decides to surprise her by picking her up at around 12:30 p.m.

Lindsey watches two new clients enter Markita office waiting to buy a house. She hears the phone ring then picks it up on the third ring. "Hello, Fresh Interior Designs, Lindsey speaking." "This is Rei speaking." "Is Markita there?" "Yes, I will connect you." "He heard the phone ring and she picked up." "Hi baby!" "What do you want?" She sits down with smiling at the phone. "Can we have lunch together?" "Okay!" "What time can I pick you up!" "1:00 p.m." "Okay, I will be there." They click off their cell phones. Lindsey walks back to her but knocks on her white door. "What is up Lindsey!" "You have a date with Rei?" She had her hair pulled up, wearing a tan tweed suit with a white blouse and tan pumps. "Lunch!" "Have you thought about getting serious with him?" "He is a client!" Lindsey gives her this look that says so what. They talk for a while until he walks inside. "You ready?" He was wearing a pair of tan pants with white shirt. His hair was pulled into a ponytail. She puts her hand into his as they walk out together. She slides into the passenger seat as he closes the door. He climbs into the driver seat but turns to ask her where she wants food from. "Mexican like tacos!" "Okay, I know the perfect place." He drove to this place called La Santos which was few blocks away. He pulled up to this spot where a truck spot. "I will bring you back some tacos okay." "Alright!"

They sat in the lot where this truck that serves Mexican food. He handed her a bag with six mini street tacos with meat, cheese, lettuce, tomatoes wrapped in foil. "I love you Rei!" He had a Burrito, and three street tacos. He got them a fruit punch to drink too.

They ate while listening to songs on the radio. "We get along just fine; will you go out with me to the club?" "Alright but as friends!" He agreed but he was not going to let them be lovers out of his mind. She came back to the office around 2:00 p.m. with him following her inside. "You two look good together." He had his arm around her waist. They strolled by her smiling until they walked in her light turquoise office. He pulled her into his arms to kiss her. "Friends remember!" "For now!" He left her smiling but wondering what he met by his last comment. He climbed back into his BMW then sped away. Markita walked toward Lindsey desk to see if there was another client on her list.

"Rei wants you Markita." "We are just friends!" "He wants more than friendship, and you know it." "He is not going be able to keep his hands off of you." "Do you really want him too?" She remained silent as she took a client's folder back to her desk. She still remembers how much fun they had at lunchtime.

He drives back to his house to watch some TV but could not stop thinking about Markita. You are the only woman I want at my side. He laid on his black leather couch pillow fantasizing about them being lovers. He takes a nap for an hour and a half but is awakened by a call on his cellphone. "Hello!" He sounded a little tired. "Rei, I need to see you at the club around 6:00 pm." "Alright, Mr. Carver!" "You are getting enough sleep, maybe you need to get laid." "I will be there!" He clicks off the phone. He wakes up and sits up to check the time. It was 4:45 p.m., he knew it was time to call his friend.

We are going to be lovers Markita. He picks up his cellphone to dial her. She answered after three rings. "You ready to go out with your friend?" "Am I talking to the same man who took me to lunch?" "Yes, are you going out with me?" "Yes, give me 40 minutes okay!" "Sure, friend." She clicks off her cellphone before he did. "He sounds too friendly." She drives home to home to take a quick shower. She realizes she should not pick out sometime to seductive. They are just friends even him calling her his friends was sticking in his throat. She walks into her bedroom toward her walk-in closet trying to decide what dress to wear. She knew it was not going to be red or some bright color. She decided to wear a wear a champagne color dress that gathers at the waist with a scoop neckline It hung just below the knees made sleeveless and had sequins circling the bottom of the dress and around the neck. She had on the same color ankle strap heels. Markita did not like too high heels especially when going dancing at a club. She pulled her hair up in a ponytail with a little down in the back. There was a gold clip on the side of her hair. She hears her doorbell ring as she glances out the window to see Rei. She opens the door to see him standing there wearing a black suit, white shirt, and black leather shoes. "You look so beautiful friend!" He smiled at her smiling face. "You look handsome too." "Thank you, friend!" He held her hand out as she placed her arm in his. He closes her side of the car door as she got into his car. He glances over at her at the traffic light just before parking. He could see her nervousness as they entered the club. Mr. Carver spotted the beauty with Rei as he signaled them to his back table. "Nice club!" "Yeah, it gets a good crowd." He stood up as he introduced her to his boss. He kissed her hand. He was wearing a dark gray suit with a white shirt. "I see why now the reason for your distraction." "Beautiful distraction!" He smiled at her, she glanced at Rei is staring in her direction. "You hungry my dear?" "Sure, what's on the menu, he handed her one." It was rose with gold trimming and the menu was in a Calisto font but in bold. The prices were written by hand but clearly. You could understand it and read it next to the pictures of the food items and drinks too Rei and Markita were interested in the chicken sliders, mozzarella sticks and wine coolers. They finished eating their food, after taking drinking half their wine coolers when she felt an older hand slide up and down her right thigh. Rei was sitting next to her. "You can take your hand of my thigh." She glared right in Mr. Carver's direction. He gave him an angry stare as he slides his chair back and stood up. "You want to dance?" She slides sideways out her hair to get away from him. "I am sorry for his behavior." She was slow dancing with him as he held her close. "It is not your fault." He gazes into her eyes while lowering his face to kiss her briefly. "Please Rei do not!" "I need us to be more than friends." "One more dance you want to leave?" "Yes, please!" The next dance was a fast one which brought a smile on their faces. "You dance well!" "So, do you!" The next alternated to a slow jam which he pulled her gently into his arms. "Last one!" He held her close to him with their eyes lock on each other. He walked back to his table to tell his boss good night! She remained silent until he pulled up into her driveway. He escorted her to her door but kisses her briefly. "Good night Markita!" "Good night Rei!" She closes the door realizing they both want more than friendship. He is about to leave her driveway when his phone rings. He sees it is Mr. Carver calling him. "Hello!" "Rei, I am sorry for touching Markita, but she is so beautiful." He does not say anything, just hangs up. He looks up at her window to see her staring out her blinds at him. He drives away to reach his house less than ten minutes. He takes a shower to climb into his bed but texts her that Mr. Carver apologize for what he did. She does not text back. She was already lying-in bed but just pick up her cellphone to see his text.

Test of Their Relationship

He sped away glancing at the trees around as he gets closer to Mr. Van Carver's estate. He stops at the front security gate for him then he walked into his tan den with oak trimming to see him talking on the telephone. He signaled him to sit down while hisdesk was made of Mahogany and his chair was burgundy and leather. He handed him a brown, envelope and he looked inside it to see $50,000. "This is your advancement." "You will get the other half after the job is completed." "Good!" "How is Markita?" "She is fine." "That she is." "Is there something between you two?" "Yes." "You just met her right." "Yes, we are involved." He left his office and drove past Markita's office. He could see her by the window in her office.

Markita was sitting in her office looking over some pictures of another client's house. She sensed someone was watching her and gazed out the window. Her eyes focus on Rei as Lindsey brought a glass with a dozen colorful flowers to her at 3:30 p.m. She looked at the rose mini card that says he is sorry, and it was from him. The phone rang ten minutes later. "Markita!" "Yes!" "I wanted to apologize for my behavior last night." "I accept your apology!" "I would like you to decorate a room in my home." He was talking to her in his office alone. "That's not possible." "Is it because of Rei?" "No!" "Think about it, I can pay you a large commission!" "I will think about it." She hung up the telephone still not trusting him. She buzzed into her office. "Yes Lindsey!" "You have another call." "Who is it?" "It is Rei!" She picked up the telephone. "You miss me already?" "Yes, you still picking me up?" "Yeah baby, I just wanted to hear your voice." "You are so sweet." "Mr. Van Carver called me to apologize and sent over flowers too." "Is that right!" "He offered me a job decorating his house." "Did you accept?" "No, I do not trust him." "I wouldn't trust him with you." They clicked off their telephone while both thought about his offer. Twenty minutes later Mr. Carver sent a limo driver to pick her up, she decided to climb into the limo. Rei called back to tell her to not accept his offer, but she told him that his boss sent a driver to pick her up. He climbs into BMW to race to his estate fast. He did not buy his apology. He approaches his security guard, he was reluctant to open the gate but Rei forcibly, convinced him. He put a choked hold on him when he pretended to leave. Mr. Van Carver ripped her ivory blouse but unfastened her black bra as he ran upstairs. He grabbed her arm by shoving her against the wood panel wall. He held her hands up to kissed her, but she turned away from him. He fondled her breasts. "Rei might seduce you, but I take what and who I want." His voice sounded cold as he approached the study door, heard Markita scream before kicking it opened. He saw his boss slap her as she fell to the floor. He ran over there to grabbed him by the throat. "I ought to kill you now." "I told you Markita is mine." His anger came through his tone. "She is nothing but a high price hooker." There was a harshness in his voice. "No, she is very different than those sluts you sleep with." He started to hit him but thought about her. She stood up and she ran into his arms. "If we have this discussion again, I will kill you!" He gave him the look of death. They went down the stair quickly after he removed his shirt to cover her breasts. He picked her up to carried her toward his car. They sped back to his house after she insisted being with him. He helped her undress as he placed her in bed. "You all right baby?" "Yes, thanks for rescuing me." She began crying as he held her. He took his clothes off as he laid next to her. He noticed the bruise on her cheek. "Hold me Rei!" Markita looked so sad while he held her. I should kill you he thought to himself. She laid her head on his chest as he considered ceasing his association with Mr. Van Carver. "Baby, I need you here by my side." She stared at him and a tear fell from her eye. "What's wrong baby?" "You really care about me?" "Yes, I haven't met a woman who sees me as a man." "Why, because of your race?" "Yes, that is a large part of it." "I slept with women but that is all it was." "No woman really wanted to take on society with me." "I will!" "We think alike." He lifted her right hand to kiss it. After we get to know each other better, we can get married." She had a surprise look on her face. "Yes, I want to marry you!" He put his hands on her face to kiss her. "You are so sweet!" "You bring out my loving side with you." "I would be honored to marry you." She manages a smile with her right cheek starting to bruise. "You and me!" "I have one more thing to do for Mr. Van Carver." "That will be it then it is you and me." They got up and got dressed again. He pulled her into his lap on the bed. She caressed his face and wrapped her arms around his neck. He held her and they kissed for several minutes. "I need to call in to the office." He handed his cellphone to her to call Lindsey before picked up the telephone. "I won't be back in until tomorrow." "Is something wrong?" "No, I am fine!" "Will you tell Thomas; I'm having a meeting with Rei." "All right, see you tomorrow!" "I will see you tomorrow." She hangs up the phone. Her co-worker could sense that something was wrong. She thought about stopping over later but she changed her mind.

New Beginnings &
Severed Ties

She walked downstairs with him holding his hand. He led her to her blue, soft leather couch and sat her down. "Does my lady require any nourishment." She heard an English accent and laughed at him. "It is nice to see you smile and hear you laugh."

"I keep good company." He caressed her hair and kissed her on the cheek. "Are you hungry?" "How about going out to a restaurant." "You sure you want to be seen with me." She walked over to him and wrapped her arms around his neck. "Yes, you are stuck with me." "Baby, you are a treasure worth more than gold." He kissed her. "Anything you want is yours including me." She smiled at him and stroked his hair. "I will go home to change clothes and be right back." I'll wait here for you." He kissed her before closing the door. She walked into the kitchen to get her a glass of water to drink. She touched her cheek and winced after feeling the pain. She took a piece of ice, placed it in a bag, and placed it on her cheek. She sat down for fifteen minutes and heard a knock on the door. She peeked out the blind and saw Lindsey standing there. She opened the door and gave half a smile. "What are you doing here?" "I came to see if you were all right." "Who hit you?" "It was Rei he is a jerk." "No, he just left here but he will be back." "It was Mr. Van Carver?" "I should have warned you; he has a reputation for being ruthless." "Yes, he tried to rape me." "That pig!" "Rei came to your rescue." "Yes, he saved me!" "I told you he's sweet on you!" "Yes, he is a sweet man!" "You and he got laid yet?" "Lindsey!" "Face it Markita it's time you met a good man." "Thanks, I am not desperate." "No, but do not let a hero get away either." They heard a knock on the door. She peeked out and saw Rei standing there. "Open it Lindsey." She opened the door and smiled at him. "You are Lindsey, I'm Rei!" "Come in!" He changed into a pair of blue jeans and a white T-Shirt with black tennis shoes. He had his hair pulled back into a ponytail. "My best friend had to check up on me." He kissed Markita. I told her you should have ripped that pig head off." "Just because he is loaded doesn't mean he has to act like a jerk." "I told her what happen!" He notices the bruise on her cheek. I should make him pay!" "No, it is his word over mine." "I promise you baby, he will regret the day he put his hands on you!" "You sure you want to have dinner out?" "Yes!" "Go have dinner and I'll see you tomorrow." "Let us go upstairs first." She walked upstairs with Markita and they investigated her closet. "I will help you cover up that bruise and pick out something to wear." "All right mother." "You slept with him?" Markita gave her a dumb founded look. "I know you have." She saw this jade dress and it had a right side slit. "This one!" She slips it on while Lindsey covered her bruise with makeup. She wore her hair down and sprayed on her favorite cologne Channel No. 5. They walked downstairs and he smiled when he saw her. "I'll leave you two alone now." "Nice meeting you Rei." "Nice meeting Markita's friend." He did not take his eyes off her. Lindsey walked out the door, got into her gray, 2017 Dodge Charger and drove away. "I thought we would never be alone." "Lindsey is just being a good friend." "I know but I need you." He caressed her soft shoulder length dark brown hair and kissed her hand. "You belong with me." "Maybe we could pick up something and bring it back." He stared in her eyes and agreed. "What do you feel like?" "How about Mexican." "Tacos and Enchiladas." "Are you a taco man." "Yes, I love tacos." "Me too!" "I know a great little place." They got into his car and he drove to a place downtown called Mei Rosas. They decided to eat there and stop at a video shop to rent some

DVDs. She picked out a mystery suspense movie, and he picked up a horror movie. He microwaves the popcorn as she went to her bedroom to change clothes. He put the tape in, and she walked out wearing a light blue, baby doll with her hair in a ponytail. He pulled her into his arms to kissed her. He removed his T-shirt and sat on the couch with her. They fed popcorn to one another as they watched the movie. He lay down on the couch with his feet up and she laid on him. He held her close to him. She pressed up against him on the scary parts of the movie. They would occasionally glance at each with desire in their eyes. She sat up it was 10:00 p.m. and winked at him. He stared at her after he pulled the DVD out, places it on the case then walked toward her. He leaned over to pick her up as she wrapped her arms around his neck. He put her down in front of the bed. He untied her teddy to slides it off her shoulders. He kissed her shoulders and took her hair down. She caressed his chest after he removed the rest of his clothes to lay on top of her. He kissed her lips, and she caressed down his back. He raised her arms up to kissed them. She closed her eyes when he kissed down her neck, shoulders, and breasts. He took turns closing his lips around each nipple gently. She sighed every time feeling his tongue teased her nipples then places tender kisses on her stomach. He raised up to stroke her soft hair then kissed her lips. He pushed her thighs apart then began entering as he heard sounds of her panting as he motioned inside her. She caressed down his back as he moved quickly toward her. He enjoyed how she felt when he was deep in her. She took a deep breath after passion ended. He held her as he lay down beside her. "Baby, how do I compare to your ex-boyfriend." "What do you think?" "Like there is a comparison." She smiled back at his smiling face. "You just know how to work my body right." "I love you Markita." "I knew the first time we talked that you're the right woman." "Rei, I care for you!". "I am just scare of being hurt again." "I promise to not hurt you intentionally." "I have something to tell you after I finished this job for Mr. Van Carver." She could see in his eyes that it was important. "I will be here when you tell me." He helped her out of bed to take a shower together before they climb back into bed. He held her while thinking about telling her the truth. He would not let it pull her away from him. She fell asleep in his arms. He kissed her once more. "Markita, you are my woman now." She was asleep when he made this statement. Mr. Van Carter, I am going to teach you a lesson in respecting a man's woman. He turned the light off and cuddled her in his arms. He fell asleep in minutes.

He awoke to kiss her soft lips. "You awake Markita?" "Yes, I am now!" "You sleep well baby?" "Yes, after that good loving!" "You can expect more of that when we are married." She caressed his face as they kissed briefly. He got up to lead her into the bathroom. He turned on the water before climbing into the shower together. He picked up the soap to gently rubbed it on his hands unto her body. She did the same to his body. They kissed as the soap rinse away as the water drenched their bodies. He kissed down her neck, shoulders and breasts then return to her lips. She stroked his black hair while caressed his strong, muscular shoulders. He grabbed her right leg as he caressed down it. She wrapped her leg around him as he entered her. He motioned toward her slowly as she panted in intervals. He kissed her in between her panting to their wet bodies coming together. He moved quickly against her as the friction of wetness made her take a deep breath after their passion ended. He held her tightly and they smiled at each other. "Is this better than taking a shower alone?" "Only with you!" Their eyes were locked on one another. He wrapped a blue towel around her before he carried her into the bedroom. He put her down then picked up this lotion on the nightstand. He unwrapped her towel then pour lotion on his hand as he started rubbing lotion allover her body. She wrapped her arms around his neck, and they kissed passionately for several minutes. She put on a rose silk blouse with matching suede skirt. He slides on a pair of gray slacks but before he puts a matching T-Shirt on, she caresses down his chests gently. He places his hand on her face to kiss her. She touches his face while stroking his goatee gently. He pulled his hair into a ponytail. They connected like he knew they would the first time they made love. They agreed that he would take her to work. "I see you later baby!" "You want to have lunch together!" "Yes!" "I will pick you up at 12:30 p.m." He kissed her lips briefly before she climbs out his car then he drove away. She walked into the office where Lindsey noticed the smile on her face. "Someone looks like cupid shot her with an arrow!" "Rei is so sweet!" "Yes, he is sweet on you." They walked into her office before she closed the door behind her. "You are lucky to have Rei at your side." "He wants to marry me when we get more acquainted with one another." "You as what's his last name." "His name is Rei Nakatani!" "Mrs. Markita Nakatani." "Do you love the guy?" "I am falling deep for him." "You are crazy about this man." "I can see that the way you two stare at one another." "Your ex has nothing on Rei, and you know it." "True, Rei is a gentleman."

"Our boss is in today; he asks about your new client." Thomas Warrington is the Office Manager and their boss. He is a 50 years old, White man with graying hair and green eyes who stands 5'8" inches tall. He worries about making a profit but is more concern about appearances. He walks into her office without knocking as Lindsey and her are talking about Rei. "I understand that Mr. Nakatani is a new client of yours." "Yes, he wants me to decorate his den and guest room." "Have you seen the rooms yet?" "I have seen the rooms, and I gave him some of my ideas which he likes them." "Have you discussed decorating price yet!" "No, we are going to discuss it over lunch." "Is this man serious about this or is he just interested in you." She tried not to smile over his last comment. "This is just a business deal." She smiles at back at her boss just to reassure him. "Let me know your progress on this account." "I will Thomas!" He left out the office door at noon. "He is seeing one of his clients!" "How do you know that?" "I overheard him talking to her on the phone." "Who is it?" The client, whose husband owns a fitness club." "Mrs. Parron's!" "You don't think he is." "I think there having an affair." "He's worry that you will cause a scandal, but he probably be the one." "Messing around with a woman who is involved with some rich guy." "You continue to see Rei, and you decorate his rooms. "I'm not going to tell!" "I'm going to lunch and he is picking me up!" "Have a good lunch." "Thanks!" She walked outside to see him waiting in the car for her. She climbs into the car and was greeted with a kiss. "Baby you missed me?" "Yes, always!" He took her back home after picking up two turkey sandwiches on wheat, chips and two lemonades at the deli. They ate lunch in the living room afterward made love in her shower. She had a contract made out for Rei to sign to show Mr. Warrington with prices for both rooms. He caressed her hair and face. "Do you have to go back to work?" He gave her this sad look. "Yes, but I will be home within three hours!" He gave her a smile. "I will be waiting for you baby." He drove her back to work, kissed her briefly to wink at her. She put his contract together before walking into Mr. Thomas office. He texted her to drive to his house after she gets off work. She thought about she has not drove her car since Rei rescued her. Rei's house. He unlocks his door, and they sit on his sofa before he gets up to leave. "Baby, I have a few errands to run but I will be back!" He kissed her. "You go back home to change into something comfortable." "Meet you at your house" He waited until she was gone before coming out the house. He left out his house fifteen minutes later. He was carrying the large, brown, envelope with the picture of his target with him. He had his 9-mm with silencer on it. He found the subjects home address and saw him alone. His mistress arrived five minutes after he got home. They got into her Ice Blue, 2018 Dodge Charger to drive to the motel. He watched as they walked into the room. He waited until two hours later before she drove him back home. He watched her leave and started to get out the car, but he came out. He followed him as he drove to this bar on an abandon road. He waited until he left the bar and pulled up next to his car and shot him. He shot him in the head twice before driving away. "I am done working for you Mr. Van Carver." He looked at the clock in his car. He drove back to his house and put this weapon back in its hiding place. He took a quick shower then slip on a pair of black khaki pants with a gray T-shirt. He left his hair down while driving over Markita's house. She opened the door; he walked in and closed the door. She was wearing a peach tank top with matching skirt. It had a right slit that hanged above her knees. She had a peach scrunch holding her hair in a ponytail. He stared at her and caressed her face gently. "I missed you Markita!" "I know me too!" "You got your errands taken care of?" "Yes!" He pulled her into his arms to kissed her. "You hungry?" "No, I just want to watch this other movie with you in my arms." "Is something wrong?" "No, I love you!" "I love you too!" He kissed her but placed his hands on her face. "I'll always be here for you baby!" She handed him a spare key to her house. "You trust me?" "Yes, with my life!" He placed his hand on her right cheek and kept it there. She laid her face down on his hand. They watched a movie on television. He kissed down her left shoulder to her wrist. He pushed her straps off her shoulders and kissed them. She gazed into his pretty, brown eyes and caressed his hair. He removed her tank top to fondle her breasts. He got up, went into her room, and got a sheet. He placed it on the tan carpet behind the couch. He took off his T-shirt and sat on the floor on his knees. She sat in front of him on her knees. He put his hands around her waist as she placed her hands on his shoulders. He kissed down her neck, shoulders, and breasts. She lay down as he finished undressing her and himself. He lay on top of her and caressed down her thighs. He caressed her stomach while she trembled when sex began which resulted in him locking his hands with her. Passion finished with him holding her close to him. She took a deep breath after satisfaction. "Baby, you make each time feel better and better." "Are you sure, I please you?" She climbed on top of him and kissed his smiling face. "Yes, I never been love so good." He rolled on top of her before kissing her lips fully. "Baby, I wish we could stay like this forever!" Me too!" He hugged her tightly. She sensed something was bothering him. "What wrong?" "Nothing, I just don't want to lose you!" "You won't!" He got up and pulled her up. He picked her up and carried her into the bathroom. They took a shower together before climbing into bed once more. He wrapped his arms around her, and they kissed for a while. She drifted asleep in his arms. "You are mine Markita, and no one is going to take you away for me," He moved away from her slowly to climb out of bed. He slips on his underwear as he stared out her window. He stood there for nearly 10 minutes in deep thought about making her his wife. He realized that he would have to tell her the truth. How do I tell her what I really do for Mr. Van Carver he thought? He walked into the bathroom to stared at himself in the mirror. He reentered the bedroom to climbed back in bed next to this beauty. He wrapped his arms around her then closed his eyes as sleep took over.

Death Comes Knocking

She awoke to the sound of someone knocking on the door. She put her robe on and looked out the window. She saw two White men dressed in dark blue suits which reminded her of cops. She asked who they are then they explained what their names are and showing their badges. She opened the door wondering who died after learning they were from Homicide. She sat down after they walked into the living room. "May I help you?" Ma'am, are you Markita Brahman?" "Yes!" "Do you know Thomas Warrington?" "Yes, what has happened?" "He is dead!" She started crying after Rei enter the room wearing a robe. "What's going on Markita?" "Who are you?" Detective Parkman looked at him with suspicion. "My name is Rei Nakatani." "Who are you to the lady?" "I am a very close friend!" He placed his arm around her waist, as she leaned on him. Detective Parkman and Detective Tinman glanced at one another. "Miss Brahman can you think of any reason why someone would kill your boss," "No, but he was having an affair with a woman whose lover is some rich guy." "Do you know who the woman is and the guy?" "I do not know!" "Ask Lindsey at the office." Detective Tinman handed her his business card. "If you think of anything give me a call." He was a White man with short, blonde hair and blue eyes. He stood 5'11" tall with a medium build. Detective Tinman is a White man with dark brown hair that hanged to his neck. He stood 5'9" tall with green eyes with a slim build. Detective Parkman handed her a card with his name and number on it. He kept a straight face when Detective Tinman showed him a picture of Markita's boss. It was the man he killed hours before driving to see Markita. He could not tell her that he killed her boss. "No, I never seen him before." Rei showed them to the door as she sat on the couch. She hugged Rei as he held her. "You all right baby?" "Yes, you are with me." He pulled away from her and kissed her. "I love you Markita," "I love you too Rei!" "You want me to drive you to work." "Yes, will you stay with me." "Yes!" "Let us take a shower!" He led her into the bathroom. They undress and climb into the bathtub. He turned on the water and picked up the soap. He rubbed it onto his hands and on her body. She did the same to his body. They kissed for several minutes as the water drenched their bodies. She placed her arms on his shoulders and caressed down his back. He kissed down her neck, to her breasts. She closed her eyes as the water covered their heads when they kissed again. He pressed her gently against the wall as passion took over. Sounds came from her as he kept making his point of how she turns him on every time. They had matching blue towels wrapped around their naked bodies. They knew that their need to be with one another was taking over. She brushed his hair and pulled it into a ponytail for him. He brushed her hair to kissed her. "Leave it down for me baby." She caressed his face as they walked into the kitchen together. She had her arm in his. He poured them up a glass of orange juice. They drove to the office at 9:45 p.m. Lindsey was standing in the light green hallway crying alone. "Lindsey!" She turned around to run to her." Did you hear about Thomas?" "Yes, the police came to my house?" "Hi Rei!". "Hi!" He gave her a hug. "I have something to take care of, but I will be right back!" "Come back soon." He kissed her then walked away. She sensed something was bothering him but did not push the issue. He drove to Mr. Van Carver house and security opened the gate. He drove in and rang the doorbell. The butler led him upstairs to the den. He had an angry look on his face. "You double crossed me!" You could hear the anger in Rei's voice, but his face showed it as well." What are you talking about?" He noticed the newspaper on his desk. It had a picture of Thomas on the front page.

He looked at the front page then stared at his face. "Oops, I gave you the wrong picture." "You killed the wrong man." He had a smirk on his face. "You set me up on purpose!" "It was a simple mistake!" "No, do you think you can get away with this?" He hit his hand across his desk. "You work for me, I own you!" "Markita is mine!" "You are going to pay for crossing me!" "Are you threatening me?" "I have money, I can make her disappear." Rei stood up and started tightening his fists. "You are dead!" He gave Mr. Van Carver a very cold stare. "Here take your payment and go get laid with Markita." "You come back, and we can talk about your next assignment." He took the money but threw it back at him." Keep your blood money." He walked out the door to leave his house. "You will regret it Rei." He picked up the telephone to make a call. "I have a job for you take care of." He hung up within ten minutes and smiled. He drove back to be by her side. He walked into the office, but she was looking through the files. "I'm back baby!" She walked toward him to kissed him. "I missed you!" "You want anything to drink?" "No, I just want you to hold me!" He held her for several minutes. "Where's Lindsey?" "She is sitting in Thomas's office. "Why?" "She is going through some of his things!" They sat in the office together going through the files for several hours. "You want some lunch out," Lindsey said. "Sure!" "What are you getting?" "How about a cheeseburger, order of fries and a banana shake." "Sounds good to me!" "Do you want a burger and fries?" "I'll have the same as my Markita." "You want to drive my car?" "Sure, I always wonder if it drives the same as mine." She handed her the keys, and he gave her a twenty-dollar bill. "I'll treat you two ladies!" "You are being sweet to us." "Yes!" She kissed him after Lindsey left out the door. She opened the door and almost dropped Markita's keys. She started the ignition, and Markita and Rei heard this loud explosion. They ran out the office to see her car burning up, but the driver side door blew all the way off. "Lindsey!" All you could see the red and yellow flames and black smoke up in the air. She screamed as she tried to run to the car, but he grabbed her to pull her back. "She's gone!" He held her tight as she cried on him. He knew that was a bomb and it was meant for Markita. He knew Mr. Van Carver was responsible for this incident. He had to protect her at all cost. The police and fire department came out within fifteen minutes. "What happen here!" "My best friend, Lindsey got into my car and it exploded," "Your car?" "Yes, she was going to pick us up something to eat," "Does she normally borrow your car?" "No, this is the first time she drove my car!" 'I am sorry for your lost!" "Do you have any enemies?" "No!" "Did Lindsey have any enemies that you knew of?" "No, she was well liked!" "You can see she is upset?" "It is all right!" "I want to know who did this?" "We will keep you informed!" "We can offer you some protection." Detective Parma looked at her concern. "No, Rei will look after me." "I will have a couple of uniform officers watching your house. Thanks!" They went outside but she locked the door. "Please take me away from here!" They walked toward his car and he checked it and found no wires or bombs. He drove her back to his place. He walked upstairs to his bedroom to she followed him. He pulled out a suitcase and started throwing a few clothes in there. "Where are you going?" She was distraught over what had occurred. "We are leaving town for a few days until this is settled." "Let the police handle it." "No, I need to tell you something." He stopped his sentence then turned away from her. "Tell me what's bothering you." She walked in front of him and took his hand.

She led him to the bed where they sat down together. "What is wrong you can tell me, I love you!" He caressed her face before kissing her for several minutes. "I have not been truthful with you about what I do." "You work for Mr. Van Carver?" "Yes, but not as a bouncer!" He gazed into her beautiful, brown eyes. "I was running from a club, but no guys were chasing me." "I do not understand?" She looks confused, while staring at her tear-stained cheeks. She listens to him attentively as he talks to her. "I killed a man that Mr. Van Carver hired me to kill." She stood up to turned away from him. "You are an Assassin?" "Yes, that is what I really do for him." He walked in front on her and stared into her eyes. He placed his hand under her chin to lift her face to meet his gaze. He gave me a picture of a man to kill yesterday" "Who was the man?" "Thomas, but it was a double cross!" "Why, did you do that!" She tried to move away from him, but he pulled her in his arms. "No, do not tell me anymore." She placed her hands over her ears, but he pulled her hands down to hear him. "I have to tell you all of it!" He placed his hands on her face to kiss her but did not resist him. "I love you Markita!" She was silent. "I did not kill Lindsey, but I know who did!" She tried to slap him twice, but he grabbed her hands. "No, baby!" "Lindsey was not the intended victim!" She stared at him sat down on the bed realizing what he was saying to her. "Me, why would anyone want to kill me?" "Mr. Van Carver hired someone to kill you." "I do not understand?" She was still confused about the why of it. "I went to see him, but I threw his money back in his face and quit!" "He told me that he owns me and that you belong to him." "No, he does not own you or me." "I love you Rei!" "Do you forgive me?" She caressed his face as he kissed her. "Yes!" "He is not going to stop until he kills you." "We can go to the police!" "No, they will find out about everything!" "I will take care of him myself!" He clenched his fist and stood up to see her standing in front of him. "I can't lose you now!" "We are in this together." "I don't want you hurt." She started to walk into the kitchen when they heard a car door shut. He ran to the window to peek out. He saw two unfamiliar faces dressed in suits but packing guns. He grabbed her hand as they ran downstairs to his secret room. They heard the door get kicked in and walking around upstairs. He pulled out his Uzi and loaded it. He saw the scared look on her face and kissed her. He heard footsteps coming downstairs and walking toward them. He sensed the guy was standing right there as he pulls the trigger. The gun sprayed bullets and left holes so they could see through the door. They saw a body fall to the floor. Rei knew his partner would not be far behind. He told her to stand behind him. He opened the door slowly and his partner was about to grab him. He saw his shadow and pulled a knife out his pocket. He brought his right hand up and stabbed him in the neck. She ran into his arms, and he held her. They stepped around the bodies. He led her upstairs to grab his suitcase and drove to her house. They went inside long enough for her to pack a few things. He was about to pull to his brother's house, but the police were already there. They headed in a different direction before they were seen. "What are we going to do now?" "We are going to go to my mother's townhouse." "She is out-of-town." "No one will find us there!" "If they do, I will be waiting." She knew he had a plan but was still worried for them. She leaned on his shoulder as he drove but ends of falling to asleep. "I love you, and no one is going to keep us apart." He was almost there but decided to stop at a store to pick up a few food items like ham, bread, mayonnaise, and some drinks. He saw his face on the television along with hers but hurried out of the store before anyone identifies him. He arrived at his mother's townhouse and caressed her face. "Wake up Markita!" "We are here?" "Did you have a peaceful nap baby!" "Yes!" They got out his car and walked inside the cabin. She looked around and saw a colonial style couch and glass table in the living room. The bedroom had a queen-size bed with an Aztec design on the bedspread. It reminds her of hers in her bedroom. "I like how this place is decorated!" "My mother decorated it!" "She has good taste; I like to meet her." "You will after this is all over." "I'm sure she would like to meet the woman I am going to marry!" She walked into the kitchen and kissed him. He caressed her face and stroked her hair. "My beautiful woman." He put the food in the cabinet then picked her up to carried her into the bathroom. They undress one another before climbing into the bathtub. He kissed her lips, down her neck, shoulders, and breasts. He plants tender kisses to her breast and stops at her stomach. She closed her eyes as he kissed up her body then stops at her lips. He takes his left hand, caressed down her back, and squeezes her butt. She strokes his hair. He picks her up to carry her into the bedroom. He pulls the sheet of the bed back as he lays her on it. He lies on top of her to kiss her before their passion starts as he moves slowly then quickly inside her. She locks her hands with his. She moaned his name before ecstasy left their bodies covered in sweat. He lay down next to her. "I need you baby!" "I know, I needed you too." "I promise when this is over with, we will be together." She stared up into his eyes as he talks to her. They pulled the sheets up while he held her close to him. "We will get through this baby." She laid her head on his chest for a while. She raised up to kisses him several times. She drifted asleep as he held her.

e watched her sleep peacefully and eased out of bed. He put his clothes on and walked downstairs to be on guard. He looked around the kitchen. He searched through the drawers and rigged a wire to ring a bell to the front door. This would signal him or her someone was in the house. He pushed the couch out so they would have to bump against it. He placed a nail sticking out the couch and they would get a hurting experience. He would be waiting for anyone Mr. Van Carver sent to kill Markita. She slept for several hours. She felt the bed and no Rei. She got up and took a shower. She put on a dark blue, short sleeve blouse with blue jeans. She put her dark brown hair in a ponytail. He heard her moving around upstairs. He started walking upstairs when they met on the steps. "You feel better baby." "Yes, but I miss you lying next to me." They walked downstairs together arm in arm. He showed her the booby traps he set up. "Can I help?" He caressed her face as he kissed her. "You make it hard to say no to you." She wrapped her arms around his neck, and they kiss for a few minutes. He led her downstairs to show her his old bedroom. "This use to be your room? "Yes!" "I will be back." She looked around the room then seen a queen size bed, a 25-inch television, and a tan, big couch with burgundy blinds in the windows. He started upstairs when he heard the booby traps go off. He turned around to quietly rejoined her. She saw him and he ran to her. "Someone is in the house." She clings to him as he grabbed his gun from this black cabinet. He moved her behind him and aimed it. He heard someone curse after the getting poke by the nail. They heard footsteps coming closer to their location, but it was his brother. "Do not shoot!" "I figure you were here," "Chris! " Man, you almost got clipped." "Is that Markita?" "Yes, Markita this is my half-brother, Chris." He shook hands with her. "She is pretty just as you told me." He wrapped his arms around her waist. "We are going to get married after this is cleared up." "Do you know what you will face with our mother?" "I do not care, I love her, and she loves me." "No one is going to keep me from her." "I have no problem with it, but she will." "Tough, she will get over it or will not." He kissed her. "I know you are serious about this." Sorry about the booby trap." He glanced down at his leg but saw no blood. "Who's with you?" "I'm sorry, they followed me." "He passed his gun behind him to her. She held it and saw someone come from behind Chris. "You're a hard man to find and this must be Markita." "It's a shame such a lovely woman has to be eliminated. He was wearing a black suit with dress shoes. He was a white man who looked thirty-five years old with blond hair and green eyes. "My name is Robert Stallman and "I am here to kill Markita," "No!" "Mr. Van Carver sends his regards." "If necessary, I am allowed to take you out." "You're expendable." "Come here darling, this will not hurt much." "You said no one would be hurt!" "I lied." He tried to make a move on him, but Robert shot him in the head. He was looking down when Rei signaled her. "Now Markita!" He moves to the right of her and she shot Robert. He started to pull the trigger, but Rei knocked the gun out his hand. He fell to the floor dead from a bullet to his chest. He went to hug Chris and Markita was still holding the gun. He stood up and removed it from her hand. "It is all right baby!" He held her in his arms. "I am sorry about your brother!" "I am too!" He was already dead. "When is this going to be over with." "Soon!" He led her upstairs into the kitchen. "We better go but they come back." "Why?" "I am, we are going to finish this once and for all." "You're not talking about facing Mr. Van Carver, are you?" "Yes, face-to-face." "We are going to settle this once and for all." He picked up the telephone to dial his number. "Hello!" "You failed!" "I do not know what you're talking about?" "Cut it out let's settle this once and for all." "Since were talking straight forward bring Markita with you." "I will!" He clicks the talk button off on the cordless telephone. "You know he will be waiting for us." "I know but I have a plan." "If I go in you can create a diversion. "No, I will go in and you sneak in and create a diversion from the outside." "I will not let you face him alone." "I will carry me some pepper spray if he gets too close." "I'll teach you a quick martial art move." "Teach me, he is going to try something." "I will kill him this time if he lays his hands on you." She caressed his face and kissed him. "I love you Markita!" "I love you too!" He taught her two moves. He tried to grab her from behind and she thrust her elbow back to his stomach. He pretended his stomach was hurting. She took her foot and pretended to step on his foot. He pretended to lean against her, and she maneuvered her knee up to his groin. "You do not want to hurt me." "No, just Mr. Van Carver." "He is going to pay for killing my best friend, Lindsey and Mr. Thomas." "He will pay for trying to rape you." "I will not allow him to hurt the man I love." "He will pay more ways than one." "He is going to learn a lesson on respecting my woman and not to double cross me." "You sure you want to do this?" "Yes, you and me!" She placed her arms around his neck to give his several brief kisses. He kissed down her neck, shoulders and returned to her lips. "We have time to finish this later."

End of the Charade

They put on their coats. "When this is over, we will get married." He caressed her face as they walked toward the door. They got into his car with happy thoughts before driving toward Mr. Van Carver's house. He stopped a block and half from his house and let her get drive the car. He got into the backseat the scrunch down. His security gate man opened the gate for her and let her drive toward the house. She got out the car and walked to the door. "Well, you're here instead of Rei." "Yes!" "He came to his senses and by letting me have the prize." He placed his arm around Markita's waist as they walked upstairs to his study. He waited until they were in the house. He eases out the passenger door slowly. He poured himself up a drink and offered one to her. "No thanks, I don't drink." "You are a pretty woman; I can see why he wants you." "I'm sure you're good in bed too." "I guess so!" He walked toward her and kissed her, but she did not resist. "You are learning why fight it." "I can make your life a lot easier." He grabbed her as he slides his hand down her back to grab her butt. She wanted to kick him in the groin but knew she was his diversion. He sneaks in the house after climbing up a tall bush to entered through his bedroom. He looked around the room and noticed a mirror above his bed. "Your horny pig!" He started searching through his stuff. He found a miniature camera placed in his dresser. "That's how you get those women to obey you." He looked in his closet and found a secret compartment that held several videotapes. He found one with a woman's husband that he killed. He pops the tape into the VCR to watch but presses the mute button. He watches twenty seconds of it and turned it off. He placed them into a bag he had on his back and walked toward the study. He peeked out the door slowly and turned the knob slowly. She saw the knob moving and stepped in front of Mr. Van Carver. "I interest you over other women you been with." "You mean had sex with!" "Yes, I been with one other African-American woman." "She was quite lovely and liked my money as much as being screwed by me." They both smiled at each other over his comment. "I'm sure she did!" She turned toward the door and reached in her purse to grab the pepper spray. "What are you doing my dear?" "Nothing, just checking my make-up." "You look fine!" "Thanks!" She turned her back to grab the pepper spray. She sprays him in the eyes. "You will pay for that." He said screaming trying to rub in eyes, but Rei was standing in front of him. "I don't think she will?" "I knew you weren't far behind!" "What you going to do kill me?" He was still trying to clear his eyes. "Maybe, but I am sure the police will be interested in your blackmailing for sex games." "You saw my tapes." "Yes, and I hid them so I can pick them up when we leave here." "You won't leave this house and Markita will be my sex toy until I get tired of her." His security guard, Stanley came in the room and he pointed a gun at her head. "You should have never double crossed me!" "Maybe, I will let Stanley have some fun with Markita first then I will join in on the fun." "You pig!" "Touch her and die!" "Still carrying on over her." "She must have been very good in bed." Stanley places his hand on her left breast and fondles it. She pulled away from him. "She has spunk!" "I like that in a woman." "I like breaking that out of a woman who resists then I make them mine." He caressed her right cheek. "Make sure you save me some to enjoy." "When I am through, she will do anything you want her to."

Turn the Tables

He raises the gun and aims it at Rei, but he kicked it away. She elbowed him in the stomach, and he bends over. Mr. Van Carver tried to rush him, but he hit him in the face. She took her pepper spray and aimed into his eyes. He grabbed his eyes and she kicked him in the groin. He fell to the floor taking turns grabbing himself and rubbing his eyes. He was cursing at her while the pain hit his eyes. "You tried to rape my woman, killed her best friend and double crossed me." "It was a misunderstanding. Markita picked up the gun and held it on Stanley. Rei grabbed him by his collar and lifted him off the floor a little. "I should kill you now." "I told you that Markita is mine." He pulled his left hand back after making a fist and hit him. He let him drop to the floor. He picked up the telephone and called the police. He made him write a confession that stated that he hired Robert Stallman to kill Markita and Mr. Thomas after she refused his advances. Rei and Markita waited for the police. Detective Tolman showed on the scene with his partner and several uniform officers. He explained how he tried to kill her after she rebuffs his advances on her and him. He handed him the bag with the videotapes to him. "Where were you on the night Mr. Thomas was killed." "I was with Markita all night." "Is that correct Ms. Brahman?" "Yes, he was with me all night." "You two can go but I want a statement tomorrow morning." They got into his car to drive back to his house. He led her upstairs to his bedroom and sat on the bed. "You didn't have to lie for me." "I know that, but I love you and can't lose you now." "I love you, but I do not want you involved with this." He caressed her face and before he kissed her passionately for several minutes. "I will not go away that easily." "I need you as my wife, Markita." "I want that too." They undress before letting the water drench them as passion conquer them with love is the focus. "You're my woman Markita." He carried her into the bedroom, while at the same time they dried one another off. They climb into bed where he held her close. He stared at the clock on his nightstand, and it read 10:45 p.m. "Where do want to go to get married?" "I do not care as long as we are together." He kissed her briefly. "Baby, we are one!" "Markita, I will make and keep you happy." She was already asleep. He caressed her right cheek and stroked her soft brown hair. He held her as he drifted asleep within minutes. She awoke to kissed him on his lips fully. He opened his eyes with a smile on his face. "You have a good sleep baby?" "Yes, always with you next to me." "You can count on that every day when we are married." He led her into the lemon color bathroom where they took a shower together before they got dress. There was a knock on the door around 11:00 a.m. He walked downstairs to the door and peeked out the curtain to see Detective Tolman standing there. He opened the door, he walked in, and he was not smiling. "What can I do for you Detective?" She came into the living room and Detective Tolman stared at her. "Is something wrong?" "No, I just wanted to tell you that we have enough evidence to convict Mr. Van Carver for a long time." "Do you still need my statement?" "Yes, I can take it now if you like." "Sure!" She answered his questions as Rei was waiting to be arrested but he just answered his questions too. "Did you notice how he looked at me?" "Yes, what does it mean?" "I think he suspects I killed Thomas, but he let it goes to convict Mr. Van Carver." "Or maybe he thinks you deserve to be happy." "Possibility but I am happy we are together." Mr. Van Carver was convicted for attempted murder on Markita and Rei, drugs, black mail. Markita left out the part of his attempted rape and gave him an alibi for Thomas murder.

They relocated to Maui where they got married in a small chapel with only guest invited was his mom. She accepted her daughter-in-law to her only son.

He still had $250,000 left from the jobs he did for Mr. Van Carver in a secret account. Rei, and Markita had $300,000 from her Interior Designs gigs and commissions. They put their money together to invest and buy property to open a Real Estate office named Surf N Interior Design/ Real Estate. She helps run the company with Rei handling the finances along with one person they hired for an Office Manager and one License Real Estate person. They were the proud parents of a baby boy who weighed 6 pounds and 21 inches. Rei chose the name Kaori which means strong he looks like Rei but has Markita eyes.

This island represents the ending of Markita and Rei life together. Their happiness that they have search for with that one special person. Their love proves how strong they are together working as one. Rei found Markita will stand by him through adversity against all odds. You do not choose who you fall in love with or when love enters your life. Sometimes you may not know if you should take a leap of faith to let love happen.